Snatch

by **Sue Hall**

AWARD PUBLICATIONS LIMITED

Snatch is a brown dog.

He has a white tip to his right ear, two white front paws, and a white tip to his tail.

Snatch doesn't like being brown. He wishes he was spotted like his Uncle Butch, whose photograph hangs on the wall. Maybe someone could paint spots on him, but that might be rather messy!

Most of all he wishes he had a collar, then he would look more like Uncle Butch.

Snatch hated being plain brown. It made him feel sad so he hid in the house. When he peeped out of the window at the other dogs he wouldn't let them see more than his eyes and nose, and they just stared back at him. They are all so different, thought Snatch.

There was Bruce who was big and patchy with a green collar; Bob, who was small, ginger and white and wore a smart black collar; Rug, a woolly grey and white dog with a red collar; a small white dog with pink edges and a blue collar who was called Bill; and Angus who was black and wiry-looking and had a tartan collar.

And then there was the hairy dog they called Frond. Even she had a big red bow round her neck, which was just as well because Snatch wasn't sure which was her back and which was her front, or even if she *had* a back or a front!

His friends, Mark Mouse and Smutty the Cat, felt so sorry for him. What could they do to help Snatch? Then they remembered the dressing-up box!

"We might find something in there for you to wear, Snatch," they said. "Maybe even a hat or a jacket."

They dug deep into the box and right at the bottom they found a colourful spotted jacket.

"What about this, Snatch?" said his friends. "Put it on and see how you look."

After a great deal of twisting and turning, Snatch finally managed to get his front paws in the right places. His little friend Mark Mouse fastened all the bright yellow buttons.

Snatch didn't really think that the jacket was a 'dog' sort of thing, but his friends said he looked very smart now that he was spotted, and the other dogs would be bound to like him.

He couldn't wait to go out and show Bruce, Bob, Rug, Bill, Angus, and even Frond – that is if he could find the right end of her!

The other dogs were so surprised to see Snatch wearing a bright spotted jacket that they all just sat down with a thump, except for Angus who was from an old Scottish clan, and had been taught to face danger on all four paws!

"Whatever is that?" said Bruce, covering Bob's eyes. Bob was always a bit afraid of strange things.

"I think it's the dog who never comes out to play," said Angus. "But he's wearing a funny spotted rag."

Snatch's eyes filled with tears and he slowly turned round and walked back to the house.

"This is the worst day of my life," he said as he sat down.

That night, when he went to sleep, Snatch
dreamed about being different...

His dreams were so real that
he twitched and jerked and
kept poor Mark Mouse awake.

He dreamed that someone
had cast a magic spell
on him and he had
been taken to a
far-off land…

…where dogs could be any colour they liked and
wear anything at all.

When he woke in the morning Snatch heard all the birds singing outside. For some strange reason he felt much happier. He had had a very strange dream last night but yet it seemed so real.

He felt a little different somehow, but it wasn't until he looked in the mirror that he saw why!

It must have been a magic dream after all! For there, round his furry brown neck, was a *bright red collar,* and hanging below the buckle was a shining golden tag with a big 'S' for Snatch on it.

Snatch was so excited!

Snatch wondered what the other dogs would think of him now...

He peeped out of the window to see if they were around. Had he frightened them all away with his spotted jacket?

"There they are!" said Mark Mouse. "They're hiding behind the tree."

Snatch went outside to show them his new red collar. One by one they came out from behind the tree. They were pleased to see Snatch looking so happy and gathered round to admire his new collar with its shining tag.

"Now," said Angus in his Scottish accent, "we hope that you will come and play with us, but you didn't need to dress up in funny clothes or wear a new collar. We wanted you to come out to play with us anyway."

They all agreed that Snatch looked very smart in his new red collar, and Snatch was so proud to play with his new friends.

ISBN 0-86163-729-1

Text and illustrations copyright © 1993 Sue Hall
This edition copyright © 1993 Award Publications Limited

First published 1993 by Award Publications Limited,
1st Floor, Goodyear House, 52-56 Osnaburgh Street,
London NW1 3NS

Printed in Belgium